Baby Love

written by
Angela DiTerlizzi

illustrated by
Brooke Boynton Hughes

Beach Lane Books New York • London • Toronto • Sydney • New Delhi

*R*osy cheeks.
Button nose.

Little fingers.

Tiny toes.

Sweet kiss.

Warm hug.

Yes, it must be baby love.

Precious smile.

Chubby thighs.

Perfect ears.

Sleepy eyes.

Sweet kiss.

Warm hug.

Yes, it must be baby love.

Soft blankie.

Snuggly bear.

Lullaby.

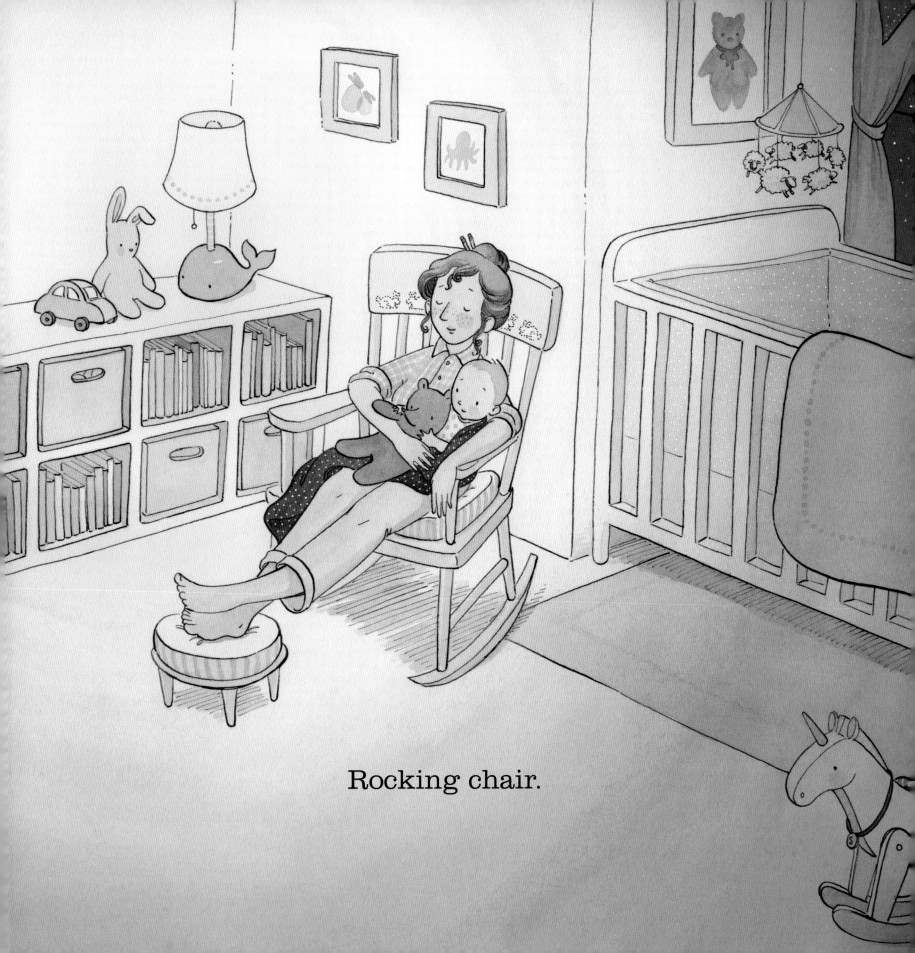

Rocking chair.

Sweet kiss.

Warm hug.

You'll *always* be our baby love.

For beautiful Baby Anna, who I hope to soon hold,
and sweet Baby Jack, who I held first—A. D.

For Mom and Dad,
with love—B. B. H.

BEACH LANE BOOKS • An imprint of Simon & Schuster Children's Publishing Division • 1230 Avenue of the Americas, New York, New York 10020 • Text copyright © 2015 by Angela DiTerlizzi • Illustrations copyright © 2015 by Brooke Boynton Hughes • All rights reserved, including the right of reproduction in whole or in part in any form. • BEACH LANE BOOKS is a trademark of Simon & Schuster, Inc. • For information about special discounts for bulk purchases, please contact Simon & Schuster Special Sales at 1-866-506-1949 or business@simonandschuster.com. • The Simon & Schuster Speakers Bureau can bring authors to your live event. For more information or to book an event, contact the Simon & Schuster Speakers Bureau at 1-866-248-3049 or visit our website at www.simonspeakers.com. • Book design by Lauren Rille • The text for this book is set in Clarendon. • The illustrations for this book are rendered in pen and ink with watercolor. • Manufactured in China • 0115 SCP • First Edition • 10 9 8 7 6 5 4 3 2 1 • Library of Congress Cataloging-in-Publication Data • DiTerlizzi, Angela. • Baby love / written by Angela DiTerlizzi ; illustrations by Brooke Boynton Hughes. • p. cm. • Summary: Illustrations and rhyming text reveal the special love between a parent and baby, from button nose to tiny toes. • ISBN 978-1-4424-3392-2 (hardcover) • ISBN 978-1-4424-3393-9 (eBook) • [1. Stories in rhyme. 2. Babies—Fiction. 3. Parent and child—Fiction.] I. Hughes, Brooke Boynton, illustrator. II. Title. • PZ8.3.D6238Bae 2015 • [E]—dc23 • 2013046179